THE STARLIGHT WATCHMAKER

THE STARLIGHT WATCHMAKER

WREN JAMES

UNION SQUARE & CO.
NEW YORK

NEW YORK

UNION SQUARE & CO. and the distinctive Union Square & Co. logo are trademarks of Sterling Publishing Co., Inc.

Union Square & Co., LLC, is a subsidiary of
Sterling Publishing Co., Inc.

Text © 2019 Wren James
Cover illustration © 2019 studiohelen.co.uk

All rights reserved. No part of this publication may be reproduced, stored in a retrieval system, or transmitted in any form or by any means (including electronic, mechanical, photocopying, recording, or otherwise) without prior written permission from the publisher.

First published in Great Britain in 2019 by Barrington Stoke Ltd.
First published in the United States and Canada in 2025 by
Union Square & Co., LLC.

ISBN 978-1-4549-6038-6

Library of Congress Control Number: 2024946373

For information about custom editions, special sales, and premium purchases, please contact specialsales@unionsquareandco.com.

Printed in Malaysia

2 4 6 8 10 9 7 5 3 1

unionsquareandco.com

Cover design by Melissa Farris

Union Square & Co.'s EVERYONE CAN BE A READER books are expertly written, thoughtfully designed with dyslexia-friendly fonts and paper tones, and carefully formatted to meet readers where they are with engaging stories that encourage reading success across a wide range of age and interest levels.

To Sarah—for being there since the very beginning and keeping pace with me every step of the way

CHAPTER 1

Hugo picked up a tiny golden cog with his tweezers just as someone rapped hard at his door. A voice yelled, "Hey, watchmaker? Open up, will you?!"

Hugo jumped with surprise and dropped the cog onto the desk. It rolled away and tumbled to the floor, falling into the crack between two floorboards.

Hugo sighed. The cog was the size of a grain of sand. He would never find it again.

"Come in," Hugo called out. He twisted his magnifying lens back into his eye socket, folding it out of sight so that only his smooth outer casing was on display. He did this because sometimes people were distracted when they could see Hugo's moving parts. It was easier for them to talk to him when he looked like a biological person too. He'd been told that the metal cogs and valves inside his robotic body were disturbing.

The door of Hugo's attic room was pushed open. It banged against the wall, and a cloud of plaster dust fell from the ceiling. A student barged in, wearing the crisp red uniform of the final year students.

"Are you the watchmaker?" the student asked with gritted teeth.

"That's me," Hugo said and folded his hands together on the desk. He tried to look calm. He hardly ever spoke to the students of the academy, despite working on the campus.

"You're an android," the student said, surprised. "I was expecting ... Oh, never mind." The student pulled the jacket of his uniform straight. The red was very bright against his green skin.

Hugo wondered which planet he came from. The academy taught children from the richest families across the galaxy—those who could afford to send their sons and daughters to another planet for school. The students were the future leaders of their planets. At the academy, they had the chance to mix with people from other places in the galaxy and learn about their cultures. It was supposed to encourage peace and understanding between the different planets.

"How can I help you?" Hugo said.

"My watch is *broken*, obviously," the student spat. "And my Time Travel for Beginners exam is tomorrow! You have to fix it."

That explained why the student was so angry. But a broken watch was something that Hugo could fix. Especially a time-travel one, which was a lot simpler than some of his other devices. Once the watch was working, this student would leave, and Hugo could be alone again. He was much happier when he was on his own.

Hugo dipped his head and said, "I'm so sorry about that. Do you have the watch with you now, Mister ... ?"

The student dropped a plain gold watch on the table. "I'm Duke Dorian Luther of the star system Hydrox."

Hugo tried not to react. He hadn't been around any nobility since his last owner, the Earl of Astea, had left him behind on this planet.

"I'm Hugo," he replied, taking a closer look at the watch.

There didn't seem to be anything wrong with it on the outside. Tiny time-travel watches such as this one looked very plain and boring, but inside they were a complicated mix of layers of cogs and gears. They were very delicate and easy to break.

Most of the students who bought these watches probably didn't even know what was inside. They just knew that if they twisted the dial, the watch would send them back in time for a few seconds. It was apparently handy when they embarrassed themselves at a dinner party or said the wrong thing during an important political meeting.

"I'm going to have to open the watch up," Hugo told the duke. "Would you like to come back in an hour?"

"I'll wait," the duke said as his antennae trembled. He was clearly annoyed. "I only bought it last semester. Are all your watches this poorly made?"

Hugo sighed and replied, "I really am very sorry. Would you like a cup of tea?"

The duke nodded stiffly and watched as Hugo filled a battered copper kettle with water and put it on the stove to heat up.

"Please, sit," Hugo said, and gestured to an armchair. It was buried under a stack of half-finished projects. Most of Hugo's attic workshop was filled with boxes of gears, stacked up in tottering piles along the walls.

The duke began to clear everything off the armchair, holding up each object and looking at it carefully. A broken cleaning spider wriggled its legs as the duke gripped it. Hugo had been meaning to fix the spider, but he had been swamped with work lately. It would soon be the end-of-term exams, and every student who had been putting off buying a watch for class had rushed to place orders.

The kettle sang out as it boiled. Hugo poured hot water over dried flowers in a teacup. The flowers unfolded and bloomed in the heat, turning the water a gentle pink, then green, before settling on purple.

"I'm sorry," Hugo said to the duke. "I don't have any sugar. I rarely have guests."

"Without is fine," the duke replied. He was looking at the pull-down mattress on the wall and the piles of spare parts. The bridge of his nose wrinkled just a bit, as if he was disgusted. Hugo felt a bit embarrassed about the state of his room.

Hugo sat back down to work. He could tell that the duke was already getting impatient by the way he was fidgeting in his seat.

But the duke stopped fidgeting when Hugo extended a screwdriver from the end of his thumb. Hugo guessed he had never seen an android use their tool attachments before. Hugo knew that biological people didn't have anything like that, and he thought it must be strange to have to get up and find whatever you needed to use. It was so much more handy to have the tools stored inside your body like androids did.

Hugo focused on opening up the back of the watch, trying very hard to ignore the duke. He loosened the screws holding the watch together.

As he worked, clockwork moths hovered around Hugo's head, glowing with light. He'd designed them to help him see inside the dark centers of the watches.

As soon as Hugo opened up the back of the watch, he saw the problem. The glowing heart of the watch was gone. There was no yellow ball—the quantum energy that powered the time travel was missing.

Hugo darted a look at the duke. He was drinking his tea and swatting at a clockwork moth sitting on the tassels of his uniform.

There was nothing but a black space below the watch's golden gears and cogs. Hugo removed the largest cogs, trying to pretend that everything was normal. His mind raced with questions as he tried to understand what had happened.

Maybe the quantum energy had slipped down inside the watch? It couldn't just have vanished into thin air. Hugo had never seen anything like this before.

The duke shifted, crossing and re-crossing his legs. "Any sign of the damage?" he asked.

"Not yet," Hugo said.

Hugo unscrewed another gear. He wasn't sure what he was going to say to the duke, who was already furious that his watch had broken. He wouldn't be happy if Hugo said he couldn't fix it.

Hugo dropped a cog onto the desk and then stopped. There was something on the back of the golden cog. He pulled out his magnifying lens from his eye and bent down to look at it. It was a small curl of green metal, stuck in the teeth of a cog.

Hugo lifted the metal free with a pair of tweezers and held it up to the light. It was the shiny green wing of a clockwork beetle.

"Ah, this is your problem," Hugo told the duke. "It's not broken. Someone has damaged it on purpose."

The duke sat bolt upright. "*What?!*" he shouted. "You mean—it's sabotage?"

Hugo beckoned the duke closer and held out the wing. "Whoever did this used a bug to take out the quantum energy that powers your watch.

Perhaps it was another student with a grudge against you?"

The duke stared at Hugo, folding his arms and creasing his perfectly ironed uniform. "Fix it," the duke said. "I need it for my exam."

Hugo had known the duke would demand this. "I can't," he replied. "I'm sorry. I don't have the parts."

The quantum energy that made the watches work was very dangerous. Hugo wasn't allowed to store it in his attic. He had to order the energy for each watch he made.

"I say, this isn't acceptable," the duke said. "You have a room full of parts. How can you not have the one I need?"

Hugo folded his magnifying glass back into his eye. "The energy is rather explosive," he explained. "I can't keep it here in case it gets hot. It could blow up the building. I can't fix your watch. I really am sorry. I can give you back the money you paid for it instead?"

"Money?!" yelled the duke. "I don't want my money. I want to be able to take my exam!"

Hugo rubbed his brow. He hated it when people shouted. They seemed to do it so often. He liked it much better when he was left on his own to work on his watches in peace. Sometimes whole weeks could pass by where Hugo didn't speak to anyone else, biological or android.

"Maybe you could find the person who broke your watch and ask for the part back?" Hugo suggested. "It's a small glowing ball of yellow energy."

The duke's eyes narrowed. "I know exactly who did this. Lady Ada de Winters. She's been angry with me ever since I took the credit for our joint coursework project in our Hyperspace Mathematics class. Ada would love it if I failed my exam."

Hugo nodded politely. "I hope she gives you back the energy," he replied. "I'd be happy to reinstall it if you find it—free of charge."

"You're coming with me," the duke said to Hugo. "I'll need you to fix the watch as soon as we find the ball of energy. I don't have time to come back out here. Why do you work on the farthest edge of campus, anyway? It's almost the wilderness."

The attic room was all that Hugo could afford to rent, but he didn't say that to the duke. "Very well. I can come with you, if you insist, duke."

"Oh, do call me Dorian," the duke said.

Hugo clicked his fingers to call his clockwork moths, and put them in his pocket along with the pieces of the duke's watch. He stood up. "Lead the way, then, Dorian," Hugo said.

CHAPTER 2

Hugo and Dorian walked across campus together to find Lady Ada de Winters. The pathways between the buildings were busy with students, and they distracted Hugo from walking. He had to focus on his feet so he didn't trip.

"What's wrong?" Dorian asked when Hugo stopped. He was watching a large, elegant butterfly ride a penny-farthing bicycle across campus. The butterfly's green hat told Hugo that she was a third-year student.

The butterflies were one of the most peaceful races in the galaxy, so they ran the public spaceships that linked all the different planets. This student on the bicycle would probably be the captain of her own spaceship when she graduated.

"Do come on, won't you?" Dorian said, tutting when Hugo still hadn't moved.

"I don't leave my room very often," Hugo explained with wide eyes. It had been so long since he'd last come outside that everything felt too busy and fast for him. There were so many people, all moving in different directions in a dreadful rush. It was nothing like Hugo's room, which might look messy, but actually had everything in its place. Out here, there was so much going on that Hugo couldn't keep up.

"Why do you hide away up there?" Dorian asked as they carried on walking. "I see android servants and caretakers sitting together in the cafe sometimes. Do you not spend time with them?"

Hugo shook his head and said, "Everything is too . . . expensive. Maybe in a few years I'll have the savings to afford that kind of thing. Until then, I have to work."

In fact, Hugo was trying to save up his money for a new zoom-in eye that would make it easier to work on small clockwork pieces. It was taking a long time, even with Hugo working all hours of the day and night. He only stopped when his systems overheated. Then he had to lie in his pull-down bed for a few hours, waiting for his cogs and gears to cool down.

"I suppose this *is* a very expensive planet," Dorian admitted. "The prices are high because the students here are all so wealthy. My home planet is much cheaper. My father owns the food supply there, you see. His taxes are much more reasonable than the ones here."

Hugo made a small mumble of understanding, while trying to hide his shock. Dorian's father controlled a whole planet's food supply? Hugo's old master, the earl, had been rich, but not *that* rich.

"Are those tattoos?" Dorian asked, pointing at Hugo's arms.

A few years ago, Hugo had been tattooed with a pattern of vines curling over his forearms. One of his customers had asked him if she could practice her tattoo designs on him before her exam. Hugo hadn't been able to resist. She'd gotten a perfect score.

"They're beautiful, aren't they?" Hugo said, showing Dorian the design with pride. "I want to get a real plant some day, when I can afford it.

I like how plants grow and change all on their own, with just a bit of care. They're so *alive*."

Dorian reached out to touch Hugo's tattoos but dropped his hand, surprised, when the plant moved under his touch. A flower bud was opening up into a blossom.

"It's made with special ink that uses my power source to move around the surface of my body," Hugo explained.

"That's wonderful." Dorian touched the tattoos again, making another flower open up.

Hugo pulled his arm away, embarrassed. The flowers normally only opened up when he was very happy. Maybe Hugo was spending too much time on his own, if he was this excited to be talking to someone new.

"Can biological people get them too?" Dorian asked.

Hugo nodded. "Some of you can. But I don't think they'd work for your species because your skin is full of green chlorophyll. It works best on metal."

"You're so lucky," Dorian said, with envy in his voice. "Sometimes I wish I were an android."

"Huh?" Hugo blurted out, surprised. "I mean, really?"

Androids were built to serve biological people. Sure, there were a few planets where androids were equal to biological people, places on the outskirts of the galaxy. But those planets were looked down on by the rest of the galaxy. Everyone said that they were doomed, headed toward riots, poverty, and wars. Hugo had always disagreed with that idea. He thought it would be nice to live in such a place.

Dorian nodded and said, "I'd definitely be an android if I could. Biological people are so fragile. We can die really easily. But all androids need is some spare cogs and light from the stars to charge your solar batteries. You could live forever."

Hugo tilted his head. Dorian was right, but he seemed to be forgetting something.

"Androids are fragile too," Hugo said. "If we *don't* have any spare cogs, when something breaks, we shut down, just like that. Then we have to hope that someone is around to fix us."

Dorian waved this off. "You've got owners to make sure that doesn't happen."

"I don't have an owner," Hugo said. "I have to look after myself. If I couldn't afford spare parts or couldn't get starlight during the day to power my solar panels, I'd be a pile of rusting metal in my attic by now."

Dorian scrunched up his face. He was silent for a moment. Hugo wondered if this idea was new to him. Had Dorian really never thought about what happened to androids without owners?

"I hadn't really considered that side of things," Dorian said at last, sounding thoughtful. "But I'm still jealous that you can change your face and hair and body whenever you want! How fun is that? Whenever there's a new fashion, you can change your look, just like that." He snapped his fingers.

Hugo looked down at his tattoos, which were still spiraling around each other. "I suppose that is fun," Hugo said.

He wondered if he had been wrong about Dorian. When he had first stormed into Hugo's attic, Hugo had assumed that Dorian was looking down on Hugo for being an android. But perhaps Dorian had just been scared and angry that his watch had broken right before his exam. Maybe Dorian hadn't been disgusted by Hugo at all. He might even see Hugo as a real person, as if he were biological. A cog fluttered somewhere inside Hugo's chest.

"Anyway, here we are!" Dorian said. "Lady Ada de Winters spends all her free time in the gym. She's probably at the climbing wall—that's if she's not hiding away somewhere, hoping I don't find her."

Hugo had never been inside the academy gym, which cost more money than he earned in a month. To Hugo's relief, Dorian paid the entry fee for them both.

Dorian led them straight to the climbing wall. The fake cliff face was at least five stories high. It stretched way above them. The rock wall bent and flexed as students pulled themselves upward using the handholds. It sometimes pushed outward, making a student lose their grip. They'd tumble several feet to bounce down onto a soft mat that absorbed the force of the fall.

"The climbing wall works in four dimensions," Dorian explained. "Not my cup of tea, but Ada loves it."

As Dorian spoke, the wall folded inward, sucking a student inside. The student was spat back out on the far side of the room, managing to keep a grip on the wall using all eight of their hands. Then the student carried on climbing.

"Which one is Ada?" Hugo asked.

Dorian grinned. "That's her." He pointed to a person whose scalp was covered in tentacles. She was using the tentacles to hold on to the wall, which was pulsing back and forth as it tried to throw her off.

Hugo was impressed. "She's very good at climbing." The wall was twisting harder as it tried to throw Ada off, but she was holding on tightly.

"Oh, no," said Dorian. "Ada's not the one doing the climbing. She *is* the climbing wall." Dorian's antennae shook as he laughed.

Hugo's jaw dropped. The wall? It was a giant rock face, as large as a building. How could that be a student?

"Ada!" Dorian called out to the rock. Hugo wondered for a moment if Dorian was a bit . . . strange. Had Hugo made a huge mistake in following him here? Then the rock wall moved, twisting to face them.

Part of the rock peeled open, and Hugo realized that it was a mouth. The two cracks above it were eyes, and two bits higher up might be ears. There was . . . there was a face on the side of the rock. The rock was alive.

"Dorian," the rock said in a creaking, groaning voice that sounded like an avalanche. "Give me one moment to finish this climb."

"Of course," Dorian said, and folded his arms behind his back.

"Which world does Ada come from?" Hugo whispered, his eyes fixed on her. She looked like a mountain. Hugo knew it was very rude to stare, but he was unable to stop himself. He'd never seen anyone like Ada before.

"Her mother is the planet Zumia," Dorian said.

"She's from Zumia?" Hugo asked.

"No, Ada's mother *is* Zumia. Ada is a young island, just a few centuries old. As she gets older, she will get bigger and bigger until she can't move around anymore. She will settle down on a planet somewhere, growing until she's a continent. After a few more million years, she'll split off and form her own planet, like her mother."

Hugo stared at the huge student. One day Ada would be so large that people would *live* on her. It seemed impossible.

Biological people came in so many different shapes and sizes that Hugo couldn't keep track of them all. They were nothing like androids. It was easy to tell where an android came from, just by looking at them. There were only a few different android models. When cogs got smaller and faster, then the androids could be upgraded to better models. That was much less complicated than all these impossible biological races. There were no rules controlling their forms at all. Just when Hugo thought he understood how they worked, he'd learn about another species that broke all the rules completely.

The student with tentacles reached the very top of the wall and dropped down onto the mat, doing a somersault as she fell. Once the student had stood up, the rock—Ada—walked over to them across the mats. Ada left behind a huge gap in the climbing wall where she had been standing.

"Hugo, this is Lady Ada de Winters," Dorian said. "Short for *Adedeneumdora*, a traditional name on her planet. Ada, this is my new friend Hugo. He made the watches for our time-travel class. He's very good."

"It's nice to meet you, Ada," Hugo said. Dorian was being very polite to Ada, considering that he thought she had broken his watch. If Hugo didn't know any better, he wouldn't have even thought that Dorian was angry.

"The pleasure is all mine," Ada rumbled back at Hugo. She held out a pebbled rock, which Hugo assumed was her hand. He shook it. "How can I help you, Dorian?" Ada asked.

Dorian drew in a tight breath. "My watch is broken. Hugo seems to think that it has been sabotaged. You wouldn't happen to know anything about it, would you, Ada? The time-travel exam is tomorrow, and I know you—" Dorian cut himself off. His voice had been getting angry.

Dorian took a breath, then in a calm tone he asked Ada, "Did you or did you not use a beetle to break my watch?"

Hugo was impressed. It was like watching a politician in training. He'd never seen anyone make such a polite accusation before.

Ada tilted her head, which made a sound like crunching gravel. "Why in the galaxy would I want to break your watch, Dorian?" Ada asked with an edge to her voice.

Hugo wished that he could leave. He didn't want to stand here while Dorian and Ada had the universe's most civilized argument.

"Are you saying you didn't do it to get revenge?" Dorian asked Ada. "I know you were furious when I took the credit for our coursework last week."

"I don't need revenge," Ada said. "I'll get better grades than you in the final exam anyway. The professor told me that we will have to plot our way through a black hole. You have no chance."

Dorian's antennae shook. "That's true, I really don't," he said sadly. "Well, if it wasn't you, Ada, then who could it have been?"

"I have no idea," Ada said. "I'm dreadfully sorry."

Dorian sighed. "If you aren't angry with me, could I borrow your watch for the exam? My exam is an hour before yours. We can easily share one watch between us."

"Well, I suppose," Ada agreed. "You can practice with it now if you want. I'm going to be helping out with the rock climbing for the rest of the day." Ada held out her arm, which was a pointed piece of rock, where a watch was dangling.

Dorian thanked her.

Hugo wondered how long it would take him to get back to his attic from here, now that Dorian didn't need him to fix his watch anymore. But before Hugo could say goodbye and leave, Dorian asked "Does it work in the same way as my watch?"

Dorian twisted the dial on the watch to send himself back in time a few seconds. Nothing happened.

"I say, your watch is broken too!" Dorian told Ada. "What's going on?"

Ada made a deep growling noise that vibrated across the floor like an earthquake. "What?" she said.

"Can I see that?" Hugo asked, taking the watch from Dorian. "I might be able to fix it."

Ada growled at Dorian. "Dorian, if you've broken my watch, I swear I'll—"

Dorian sniffed. "I didn't even break my own watch! I *told* you. Someone else did. It was sabotage."

"That remains to be seen," Ada said. "It seems to me that this is just the result of your own lack of skill."

Their polite tones had gone now as they became more and more furious.

"Excuse me, madam!" Dorian replied. "Hugo said the watch was broken by someone on purpose, and he's a *professional*. I hardly think you should question his expert opinion."

While they were arguing, Hugo opened up the back of Ada's watch. He released the spring and lifted up the ratchet to see underneath the gears.

Soon Ada and Dorian stopped arguing and started speaking in a rumbling language that sounded like rocks grinding together. Dorian was slow and careful when he spoke. It was clear that he was still learning the language. Ada kept repeating words until Dorian understood them.

Hugo listened to them speaking as he unscrewed another tiny cog in the watch.

"Nearly there," Hugo said, and it was only when they both turned to look at him that Hugo realized he'd said it in Ada's language.

"Wait—you know Zumian?" Dorian asked. "How did you learn that so fast?!"

"Oh." Hugo rubbed the back of his neck. "It was part of my programming for being a servant. I have to be able to understand people so I can serve them. I can pick up any language after a few minutes of conversation."

"That's brilliant!" Dorian said. "I've spent three years learning Ada's language for my diplomacy course and I'm still terrible. You should help me practice."

Hugo had been looking forward to getting back to his room and being on his own again. But to his surprise, the thought of Dorian visiting him to practice speaking Zumian didn't sound that bad. It actually might be . . . nice.

"I think I'd like that," Hugo admitted.

"What other languages do you speak?" Ada asked Hugo.

"Oh, I traveled all over the galaxy with my old master," Hugo said. "I've probably picked up around forty languages."

Ada and Dorian were both impressed.

Hugo carried on working on the watch, a bit embarrassed by the attention. He unscrewed the last cog and opened up the inside of the watch. The yellow ball of quantum energy was missing from this one too.

"Ah," Hugo said, and held up the watch for the others to see.

Dorian stared at it. "So it's not just my watch that has been a target," he said. Dorian sounded very relieved to find out that no one hated him so much that they would try to make him fail his exam.

"Someone must be collecting quantum energy," Hugo said, worried.

"Why would they take it from *my* watch?" Ada asked. She was steaming in fury, and a tiny volcano on her upper arm was spewing red lava.

"Why would anyone want that much power?" Dorian asked Hugo. "Didn't you say that it was dangerous?"

Hugo frowned. "It is. Very dangerous, in fact."

Dorian's face had gone pale. "What could it be used for?" he asked.

"Well, I suppose you could use it to power a spaceship," Hugo said. "Or . . . oh."

"What? What is it?" asked Dorian.

"You could use it to make a bomb," Hugo whispered.

CHAPTER 3

"We need to stop this. *Right now*," Ada said, her voice rumbling with fear.

The academy had been attacked before. Ten students had been injured in a bombing just a few years ago. It was a common target because the students were all from wealthy, powerful families. If someone wanted to cause a war or find a person to ransom, the academy was a good place to start. Security guards patrolled all over the campus, checking that everyone had permits to be there and that no one was planning on causing any trouble.

"Is there any way we can find out who had the chance to get at your watches?" Hugo asked.

He hadn't really been interested in finding out who had broken Dorian's watch before. But Hugo was really worried now. There could be something seriously wrong here. It might be something fairly innocent, such as sabotage against classmates just before an exam. But if there was even a chance that it was something more sinister, then Hugo felt he had to find out what was going on. He was involved now, however much he wanted to go back to his peaceful attic.

"What do you mean, find out who could get to our watches?" Ada asked.

Hugo thought about it. "Well, do you have security systems in your rooms?"

Dorian's eyes lit up. "I do!"

Ada ground her rocks together and said, "Why didn't you check your security system before you stormed in here accusing me of sabotage, you silly boy?"

"I have never *stormed* anywhere in my life," Dorian said, puffing out his chest. "And . . . I didn't think of it," he added weakly.

Hugo felt the need to hurry this along. Someone might be making a bomb right at this moment. They didn't have time to bicker. He worried that Dorian and Ada weren't taking this very seriously.

"Shall we go?" Hugo asked, and gestured to the door.

"You two go," Ada said. "I'll ask the other students in our time-travel class if their watches are broken. I might be able to find some more evidence about who stole the energy."

Dorian nodded and replied, "We'll let you know if we find anything useful."

⋅ ★ ⋅

"How did you end up working at the academy, then?" Dorian asked Hugo as they caught the steam-engine tram to Dorian's dorm. The tram didn't ever seem to stop, as far as Hugo could tell. Instead, students used handles to hold on to the outside of the tram carriages and hopped away when they wanted to get off.

"I used to be a servant," Hugo explained. "My master, the Earl of Astea, left me behind when he graduated."

Hugo tried to be casual about it, but somehow his voice ended up shaking as he spoke.

It had been awful. Hugo's whole life had revolved around making the earl happy, and then one day, just like that, Hugo had been on his own. The earl left the planet, and Hugo's whole world had shattered.

He had spent a long time wondering if he had done something to upset the earl. But he hadn't been able to think of anything really bad that he could have done wrong. Hugo had always ironed the earl's uniform as smooth as paper and polished his knee-high black boots to a gleaming shine. The earl had even joked around with him sometimes. They hadn't been friends, but Hugo didn't think the earl hated him or found him annoying. The earl seemed to like him—when he remembered that Hugo existed.

Hugo had tried to tell himself that the earl had probably just decided to get a newer, faster, shinier android model. He'd told himself that it wasn't personal. But Hugo didn't really believe that.

"The earl *abandoned* you?" Dorian asked, frowning.

"Well, 'abandoned' is a very strong word," Hugo replied. "But I suppose."

"How terrible!" Dorian said. "How did you survive?"

Hugo's cogs jolted out of sync as he remembered the fear that had overtaken him when he'd watched the earl's private spaceship take off without him. Hugo hadn't had any money, or friends, or a way to contact anyone. He hadn't known what to do.

"I couldn't afford to pay for a ride off the planet to find my way back to Astea," Hugo said. "The security guards kept trying to get me to leave the campus, because my access pass expired as soon as the earl left. I didn't have a reason to be on campus when I stopped being a servant. The guards were patrolling all the time because of security threats."

Androids weren't allowed to be at the academy if they didn't have a job. Hugo had tried to apply for a temporary permit so the guards would leave him alone, but his application was rejected. And there had been nowhere else to go. The whole rest of the planet was ocean. The academy owned all the land. With no money to travel off-planet, Hugo had been trapped.

"I was hiding from the guards one day," Hugo said, "when I ended up behind one of the science buildings, near the trash bins—"

Dorian interrupted to say, "We need to get off the tram here."

They leaped from the moving tram. Dorian landed neatly. He turned to catch Hugo, who tripped and almost fell onto the grass verge.

"Thank you," Hugo said, and pulled away. He had forgotten what he'd been saying.

"You were by the trash bins . . . ?" Dorian prompted Hugo as they walked to Dorian's dorm.

Hugo said, "I found a bag of broken cogs and gears that had been thrown away from the engineering classrooms. I kept them and taught myself watchmaking by fixing an old watch the earl had given me. I remembered how often the earl's watches broke and thought if I could repair them, I might be useful to one of the students. I was actually . . ." Hugo trailed off, feeling a bit nervous.

"Yes?" Dorian said, while nodding hello to a passing cloud of glowing mist. The cloud grew brighter in reply.

"I was hoping that a student would be so pleased that I had fixed their watch that they would hire me as a servant," Hugo said. It seemed a small and silly dream to Hugo now. None of these rich students would want a secondhand android servant. Especially one who had been abandoned without warning. Hugo must have been very terrible at his job to have deserved that.

"But instead, I started being paid to fix watches," Hugo continued. "Soon, I could afford to rent my small attic room on the edge of campus. After a while, I was able to buy some clockwork parts, so that I could start making my own watches. I've been selling them in the academy shop ever since." Once Hugo had proved that he could be useful, the academy had agreed to let him stay and work as a watchmaker.

"Well, you certainly have made the most of an awful situation," Dorian said. "Did you say your master's name was the Earl of Astea? I wonder if I've met him." Dorian frowned thoughtfully.

"He's a politician for the Terra council now," Hugo said. He'd found this out when he'd seen an article in the news about a speech the earl had given.

Dorian shuddered. "Oh, dear, the *Terra* council? What a bunch of scoundrels. Well, you're better off without him, I say."

Hugo beamed at Dorian. "I think so too."

Hugo suddenly felt strange all over. He realized with a shock that he was *happy*. For the first time in ages, Hugo felt happy. It wasn't terrible at all, talking to Dorian and getting to know him. It was actually nice.

Hugo knew then that he had been lying to himself about wanting to be back in his attic. He hadn't enjoyed being on his own. He'd been lonely, stuck up there without any company. Really, Hugo had missed other people. He *liked* being with Dorian, even if they might uncover some dangerous bomb plot together.

"This is my dormitory here," Dorian said, walking up to the entrance of a towering skyscraper. A security guard marched over to them.

"Excuse me," the guard asked Hugo. "Can I see some ID, please?"

Dorian stared at the guard and said, "What do you mean by this?"

At the same time, Hugo said, "Of course!"

Hugo was used to being asked for identification when he was alone on campus. Hugo showed them his ID card for the watchmakers' guild. The guard checked it carefully.

"That all seems to be in order," the guard said. "Have a good day, milord," he added to Dorian, completely ignoring Hugo.

Hugo followed Dorian into the elevator in silence, with his head bowed. He hadn't expected a guard to question him when he was with Dorian. It was embarrassing. Dorian had only just started treating Hugo like a person instead of a *thing*, and now he would go back to looking down on him again.

Dorian cleared his throat. "You might want to hold on," he said lightly to Hugo, just as the glass elevator shot upward at top speed.

Hugo didn't have time to reach out for the handrail. He watched the ground vanish far below them and felt a bit dizzy.

Dorian's dorm room was so high up that there were clouds outside the windows. Hugo saw a flurry of snowflakes press up against the glass and shivered.

"I have the penthouse suite," Dorian explained as he opened the door. The room was filled with an enormous four-poster bed covered in piles of fluffy pillows. There was a desk for studying, but it was hidden somewhere underneath wrinkled pieces of red uniform, dirty plates and cups, and what looked like a croquet mallet and set of wooden hoops.

Hugo took it all in, amazed. This was nothing like he'd imagined. There was even an aquarium filled with green goo by the windows.

"What's that?" Hugo asked, pointing at it.

"That's algae. It's what I eat. Don't look at the tank, it needs a good cleaning. It's embarrassingly dirty."

"Very nice," Hugo said politely, trying not to show his feelings of horror. Hugo's body ran off solar power, so he didn't need to eat anything. He thought all food looked a bit disgusting. But this watery plant looked *especially* horrible.

"This is my security system," Dorian said. He gestured toward a golden bird dozing on a perch. It had a long, swooping tail of sparkling feathers. It let out a soft coo when it saw Dorian. Its eyes were as green as emeralds.

"The . . . the bird?" Hugo asked, confused. He'd been expecting a clockwork security device.

Dorian scratched the bird's chest. It jiggled its wings in a flutter of feathers.

"I designed her from scratch myself," Dorian said. His chest puffed out with pride, his antennae fluttering.

Hugo understood all of a sudden. There were vending machines scattered around campus where you could build animals by typing out a long string of DNA code. You could decide what shape, size, and color of animal it made. The machine would print the animal while you waited.

Hugo had watched the earl try to use one of the DNA vending machines a few years ago. All he'd managed to make was a deformed one-eyed lizard. It had been a mean, miserable thing.

"She's beautiful," Hugo said, and reached out to touch the soft downy feathers on the bird's head. They were covered in fine silver swirls. The bird tilted her head into Hugo's metal palm and rubbed against him.

"Oh!" Dorian said, and pointed at Hugo's arm. His tattoos were twisting into the shape of a tiny bird. It nestled in between the tattooed flowers and vines, fluttering its wings.

Hugo hid his arm behind his back, but Dorian was smiling at him.

"I'm glad you like her," Dorian said.

"She's the most beautiful thing I've ever seen," Hugo replied honestly.

Still smiling, Dorian turned to the bird and said, "Angel, could you show us if anyone has been into my room in the last day, please?"

The bird squawked and opened her beak. A light beam came from inside her mouth and projected onto the wall. The light changed color and started moving, forming a picture of an empty four-poster bed.

Hugo realized that it was a video recording of Dorian's room. The bed was a tidier version of the messy one they were standing next to. Hugo could see the clouds outside the windows.

An android moved into view and bent down to suck up dust from the floor with a vacuum tool. The cleaner tidied up Dorian's room, emptying the trash bin, and plumping up his pillows. Then the cleaner stopped and picked up something from Dorian's bedside table. The time-travel watch.

The cleaner looked around the empty room, with a careful blank look on his face that made Hugo shiver. Then the cleaner released a green clockwork beetle onto the watch. The tiny insect scuttled over the surface of the watch and slipped into a crack in the side with a wiggle.

The cleaner looked down at the watch, waiting. There was something awful about the way the cleaner was standing, like a hungry predator waiting to take down his prey.

Hugo felt sick. He looked at Dorian and saw that he was watching the video with a frown.

After a long moment, the beetle returned from inside the watch. It was carrying a tiny yellow ball of quantum energy between its wings. The cleaner smirked, and dark shadows filled the hollows of his cheeks. The cleaner picked up the beetle and put it in a matchbox, which glowed from the light of the quantum energy.

Then the cleaner continued tidying the room, patting his pocket where the matchbox was hidden every now and then.

Hugo felt his springs pulling tighter and tighter, until he was sure they would snap. This wasn't right. Only a truly desperate android would steal like that. It was unnatural. It went against everything Hugo believed. Just looking at the android cleaner made Hugo feel ill. He felt sure that whatever the cleaner was planning to do with the quantum energy, it wasn't going to be good.

"*Well!*" Dorian said sharply. "I shall certainly be reporting this to the academy. Their staff shouldn't be stealing from the students. That's completely unacceptable."

Hugo frowned. Dorian didn't understand how serious this was at all. Hadn't he heard Hugo say that the quantum energy could be used to make a bomb?

Dorian paused the video on the image of the cleaner's face and said, "We should take this to the security guards."

Hugo winced, thinking of how the security guard had stopped him and checked his ID before. He hadn't trusted Hugo at all. If Dorian told the security guard that an android had stolen quantum energy, he would arrest Hugo on the spot. It wouldn't matter that he had nothing to do with this.

"No," Hugo said quickly. "I don't think we should tell anyone. We don't want to make a fuss over nothing. It might just be someone playing a prank. We can solve this on our own."

Hugo might lose his watchmaker's license if he drew too much attention to himself. He couldn't risk that. He and Dorian would have to solve this on their own. That would be much safer.

"I know how we can find the cleaner ourselves," Hugo continued. "Then we can confront him without getting the security guards involved."

"How?" Dorian asked.

"I know where the cleaners' staff room is," Hugo said. "I went there once for a job interview."

Dorian nodded. He fed his bird a piece of fruit and said, "Well done, Angel."

The bird nuzzled against Dorian's palm and then settled back on her perch, her emerald eyes shutting.

CHAPTER 4

"Why were you trying to become a cleaner?" Dorian asked Hugo as they waited for the elevator to take them back down to the ground floor.

Hugo pulled a face. "I tried to become a cleaner for the academy after the earl left me here. But they get hundreds of applications from other androids who lose their jobs when their owners upgrade to newer models. The academy put me on the waiting list to be a cleaner, but they said it would probably be eight years or more before they had a space for me."

"It's a good thing you started fixing watches instead," Dorian said.

"I like it a lot more than I would have liked cleaning, I think," Hugo agreed. But at least the cleaners all got to work together. Hugo was starting to realize how bad it was for him to spend so much time on his own.

Dorian and Hugo caught the tram toward the academy staff building. They were almost there when Dorian spotted Ada making her way along a footpath in a rolling, tumbling sort of walk. Dorian gestured to Hugo and jumped from the tram, landing smoothly. Hugo followed him, stumbling and nearly falling once again. Dorian squeezed his arm and said, "You'll get the hang of it soon."

"Sure," Hugo said, but he was doubtful. If he couldn't travel by walking nice and slowly, then he'd probably prefer to ride one of those penny-farthing bicycles that the butterflies used, rather than take the tram.

"Ada!" Dorian called, waving his arm at her.

She came to a stop, eventually, and turned to look at them. "Hello, gentlemen," Ada rumbled. "I found a few more people in our class with broken watches. Lady Wrath, His Honorable Beep, and Prince Fee."

"Prince Fee?" Dorian said, surprised. "He's my next-door neighbor. He's . . . very *loud* at night."

"But that makes sense!" Hugo exclaimed. Dorian turned to him with wide eyes, and Hugo clarified: "Not the 'loud at night' part. I meant, if he's in the room next to yours, he must have the same cleaner as you do. The cleaner probably stole the quantum energy from his watch too. Do the others live in your building as well?"

"Oh!" Dorian said. "Yes, they do! Beep is on the floor below me. And Ada lives on the ground floor near Lady Wrath. The same cleaner probably broke your watch too, Ada."

Hugo tried to count up the number of rooms in the skyscraper. If the cleaner had access to all of them, then he could have collected a huge amount of quantum energy by now. How much more would he need to build a bomb?

Hugo didn't even want to think about it. He still remembered how the ground had shaken the last time someone had tried to set off a bomb at the academy. He'd felt it even on the outskirts of campus in his attic. Dust had fallen from the ceiling right into the watch mechanism he was working on. And that bomb hadn't even gone off properly. A bomb with this much quantum energy might destroy the whole planet.

"Was it a cleaner who stole the energy, then?" Ada rumbled at Dorian.

Dorian puffed out his chest with pride. "Ada, that clever bird of mine recorded the thief in action. It's one of the academy's cleaning androids. We're going to see if we can track him down now. Would you like to come?"

Ada agreed, and they walked to the staff building. Hugo thought it was the prettiest place on campus. The tall buildings like Dorian's dorm were very impressive, but this small one was much better. It was shaped like a bowl and curled along the side of a river. Wind rushed around the scooped-out center of the wall and made a beautiful humming noise that sounded like music.

After the earl had abandoned him, Hugo had often stood here and listened to the building after the sun had gone down. It'd made him feel a bit happier, even when everything in his life had been falling apart. But one day, the security guards had chased Hugo away. He'd never had the courage to come back and listen to the building's noises again.

Hugo closed his eyes, listening to the sweeping music.

"What are you doing?" Dorian asked.

"Isn't it beautiful?" Hugo said, tilting his head.

"What is?" Dorian asked, confused. "Oh! The wind?" Dorian hummed. "I suppose it is a pretty little tinkling sound. I hadn't noticed before." He looked at Hugo for a moment. "I wonder if I'd notice the things you do if I spent more time hidden away in an attic."

"You do live in a penthouse room," Hugo pointed out. "That's just a fancier name for an attic."

Ada rumbled out a laugh and said, "He's right, you know."

"No, he's not!" Dorian said, offended. "Attics and penthouses are completely different! Aren't they?" He frowned. "I'm sure they are."

Hugo shook his head, pretending to be sad. "Dorian, they really aren't."

Dorian squinted at Hugo, his antennae drooping. Then Dorian let out a loud laugh.

"That was a joke, wasn't it?" he said. "You're joking with me! Brilliant!"

Hugo smiled a short, stiff smile. He wasn't sure he'd ever made a joke before. "I think it was," Hugo said.

They walked up to the main entrance of the staff building. Dorian strolled up to the automatic sliding doors, but they didn't open for him and he walked right into the glass.

Dorian backed up and waved at the doors. They still didn't open.

"Hey, guard!" Dorian called to the security guard on the inside of the entrance. "Your doors are broken!"

"Are you a student?" the guard asked. She was one of those fluffy clouds of gas that Hugo had seen around campus. Her voice was as thin and floaty as her body.

"Of course I'm a student!" Dorian declared. "I'm Duke Dorian Luther of the star system—"

"No students are allowed," the guard said, interrupting Dorian. "This is a staff building. The doors won't let you in."

Dorian opened his mouth and then closed it again.

"Are you two cleaning staff?" the guard asked Ada and Hugo.

They slowly shook their heads.

The guard's gaseous body rippled. She said, "Then please stand clear of the entrance."

They had no choice but to back away from the staff building.

"What now?!" Dorian asked, his antennae flexing with dismay.

"We'll have to find another way inside," Ada said.

"The cleaners' staff room is at the back of the building," Hugo said. "We might be able to find a way to get inside using another door."

"Oh, we're breaking in? Excellent!" Dorian said. His green skin seemed to glow with excitement as he headed for the back of the building.

Ada turned to look at Hugo with an expression of exhaustion. "Before you ask,

Dorian is always like this," Ada said. "Even during exams."

"That doesn't surprise me even a little bit," Hugo replied.

Hugo could tell that Ada was worried about the stolen quantum energy, just like him. But for some reason, Dorian didn't seem to understand the threat. He was just excited to be going on an adventure. Yet Hugo didn't want to correct him. If Dorian started panicking, then Hugo thought his own fears might overtake him too. Hugo had to focus on finding the cleaner, instead of worrying about what might happen if they didn't get to him in time.

"I've never heard of an android committing a crime before," Ada said as they walked.

Hugo made a small murmur of agreement. "It's rare."

He'd been thinking about that too. Hugo didn't want to believe that androids were capable of doing something like this. But they were people, just like everyone else. There was nothing to stop an android from setting off a bomb, if they really wanted to. It made Hugo feel awful to admit this. He was normally proud to be an android. Not today.

"I always assumed that androids were just computers," Ada admitted. "I've not really met many of you before."

Hugo made a face. "A lot of biological people find it hard to understand us," he said. "We're made of metal, but we think and feel just like you do."

"I'm sorry. I never realized." Ada looked upset.

Hugo shrugged and said, "I don't blame you. I don't really understand biological people."

"Doesn't it get tiring being judged for who you are all the time?" Ada asked. "And treated like you're less than other people?"

Hugo didn't know what to say to that. "I spend most of my time in my attic."

Ada looked at him with deep pity.

Walking at Ada's slow speed, by the time they had caught up with Dorian, he had checked the whole back of the building for a way to get inside.

Dorian sighed. "There aren't any open doors we can slip into. But, Hugo, do you know which floor the cleaners' staff room is on?"

"Er. The third, I think. Why?"

"Around the place where that open window is, would you say?" Dorian asked. He pointed to a tiny window far above them, which was tilted open to let in the air.

"Maybe . . . ," Hugo said. The thought of climbing up the side of the building was sending his gears and levers into a tizzy. It would be much easier if they could find a door.

Dorian turned to them, his eyes glowing with dangerous glee. "Ada, your climbing-wall skills are required, if you please. We're going to look in through that window."

Ada's mouth slid open in a wide, gaping grin. Hugo saw red-hot lava deep inside her throat, rolling over itself as it boiled. The small volcano on her upper arm belched out a cloud of steam.

"Excellent," Ada said.

"I'm not quite sure—" Hugo tried to protest, but Ada was already spilling lava onto the ground below her. The red-hot lava solidified into stone as it cooled, lifting Ada into the air. She released more and more lava, until she was towering over them.

They had to step back then, as the heat Ada was giving off would have melted Hugo's metal body. The lava erupted from her, making the air shimmer as it formed a tiny mountain against the side of the staff building.

"That'll do!" Dorian called when Ada had grown to the size of the second floor. "We can probably reach from there!"

Ada's volcanoes stopped leaking lava, and she settled into place, cooling down into a dark black rock. The ground beneath her had cracked from the heat.

Dorian touched Ada's base and then jerked his hand back, hissing. He blew on his fingertips.

"Still a bit hot," Dorian said.

"Does she do this often?" Hugo asked. If she could grow this fast, why had Dorian said that it was going to take her millions of years to get to the size of a planet? At this rate, Ada could be the size of a small moon by dusk. "Why isn't she bigger, if she can grow like this?"

"Ada tends to litter," Dorian explained. "Her mother won't let her get so big that she can't walk until after Ada's graduated. I think she does this to let off steam, and then, well . . . she detaches the bits of her body that she doesn't want."

Hugo frowned. "What happens to those bits?" He tried to remember if he'd ever seen any small hills of solid lava around the campus. He was sure he'd have noticed.

"The butterflies eat it," Ada rumbled down at them. "It's nutritious for their species."

Hugo grimaced, feeling slightly ill. "Delicious," he called back at Ada.

Dorian touched the lava again. It must have cooled now, because he started climbing. Hugo tested it. It was warm, but it wasn't so hot that it would overheat his cogs and make them grind together.

Hugo extended all of the tools from his fingers for extra grip on the smooth surface of the lava and started to follow Dorian.

Ada was very good at being a climbing wall. There were small ledges and foot holes at exactly the right places Hugo needed as he climbed. In no time at all, Dorian and Hugo were perched on top of Ada's head, looking in through the third-floor window.

"Is this the right one?" Dorian whispered.

Hugo squinted, trying to remember what the cleaners' staff room had looked like when he'd come here for a job interview.

"No," Hugo said eventually. "I think it's the next one across."

Ada immediately created a small platform for them to walk along. Dorian walked down it to the next window along, but Hugo opted to crawl instead. They weren't *that* high up, but Hugo was still too far from the ground to be totally comfortable. His cogs and gears were very delicate. He wasn't sure he'd survive a fall from this height.

The next room was full of people. Surprised, Hugo and Dorian both dropped down out of sight.

"This is it!" Hugo whispered. "Those were androids!" Before he'd hidden, he'd seen one of the androids washing dirt off the cleaning extensions in her fingers.

"We should see if we can overhear any of them talking about the quantum energy," Dorian said. "The cleaner from my room might have a partner. Stay down, I'll try to listen."

Dorian pressed his ear to the glass. He listened carefully and then gestured for Hugo to stand up and listen too.

Inside, two androids were speaking to each other in a vibrating, metallic language.

Dorian frowned and whispered, "Damn and blast. I don't speak Hiccaran—do you?"

Hugo nodded.

Dorian huffed. "I suppose I shouldn't be surprised. Is there anything you *can't* do, Mr. Watchmaker?"

Hugo knew by now that Dorian was teasing, and he didn't get upset. Instead, he translated: "One of them said, 'The elevator was acting up again, so you should use the other entrance next time you drop off the energy.' Then the other one said, 'Which corner of the library is it again?'"

Hugo listened some more.

"What else?" Dorian asked, too loudly.

"Shhh," Hugo told Dorian. "They said the western corner, I think. I haven't heard that word before, but that sounds about right. Now they're arranging to meet again tomorrow after they've dropped the energy off."

"What else?" Dorian repeated.

"One of them just said, 'Time is running out. If we don't pick up speed . . .' and then something about this ending in a shutdown."

Hugo frowned. He wasn't completely sure he'd translated that properly, but a shutdown didn't sound good. Were they planning to shut down the whole planet after the explosion?

"Oh, no," Dorian said, sounding dejected. His excitement seemed to melt off him as he finally realized how serious this all was.

The androids chatted for a bit longer, but they didn't say anything else useful or explain what the energy was for.

"I think we're done, Ada," Dorian called out. "Can you let us down?"

Ada lowered them back down to the ground. She started shaking and shedding stones in an avalanche, then she stepped away from the lava tower she'd made.

"Subtle, Ada," Dorian said over the roar of crumbling rocks. "You know that they *definitely* heard that."

"Then start running," Ada rumbled.

CHAPTER 5

Hugo, Dorian, and Ada went straight to the library. All of them were silent—too scared of the threat of attack to talk. Dorian and Ada used their student IDs to enter the library. Hugo hid behind Ada, so that the guards didn't see him. His ID didn't give him access to the library.

Once they were safely inside, they walked to the western corner of the library, searching for any sign of the entrance that the androids had been talking about.

"It must be a hidden entrance," Dorian said, rubbing his chin. "They said they normally take the elevator, but it's broken."

Hugo was too distracted by the library to pay attention. It had glass walls and ceilings that were dripping with moisture to keep the books watered.

The library was full of different bushes and shrubs lined up in rows. To choose a book, you walked down the stacks until you found the right plant and picked one of its flowers. Each petal unfurled to become a page, and black veins on it formed writing. The longer the book, the larger and fluffier the flower, with hundreds of petals covered in writing.

You could snip the blossom and take away the book. If you pressed the flower under something heavy, it would dry out and the book would last for years. Then the plant would grow another flower for anyone else who wanted to read it.

The western part of the library was filled with huge trees stretching up to the ceiling. A librarian was pruning the branches of one of the trees, standing halfway up a ladder that was propped against the trunk.

The librarian pulled a huge nut off one of the branches and lowered it down in a basket. The nut had raised words spiraling around the outside of its shell. Hugo wondered if that kind of book was for people who didn't have eyes.

Ada sighed, letting out a gust of steam. She touched a leaf on one of the bushes and said, "I wish I had a garden. But I need to be bigger before any plants will grow on me."

"You could get some small plants," Hugo suggested. "A moss, maybe? I could help you find some." There were some fluffy brown mosses growing on the outside of his building. He could see them when he peered out of his attic window, soaking up the starlight during the day, just like he did himself.

They carried on down the path between the trees until they reached the western corner of the library. There was no obvious sign of any doors or staircases.

"Let's split up and look," Dorian suggested.

Hugo took the right-hand path, walking past a student who was working at a desk. The desk was made out of a living tree, with four branches bending down to the floor and a flat trunk on top.

Hugo was so amazed by the desk that he almost walked right over a manhole cover set into the ground. It was only when he tripped over it that he stopped and looked down. Could it be . . . ?

Hugo knelt down and pulled out his magnifying lens from his eye. There was something caught in the edge of the manhole cover. He picked it up with his tweezers. It was another wing from a clockwork beetle, just like the one that had stolen the energy from Dorian's watch.

Was this the entrance that the cleaners had been talking about? The manhole probably led down to the watering system for the plants. Could the cleaners have been taking the energy to someone down there?

"Dorian," Hugo hissed and stuck his head between two spiky yellow plants into the next row. "Come here!"

"Have you found something?" Dorian asked, jogging over. He looked a bit ruffled. "We need to hurry up. That librarian keeps giving me dodgy looks. I think she knows we're up to something, and I don't want her to come at me with those shears." Dorian shivered and pressed a hand over his antennae.

Hugo held up the wing and said, "I think they went underground!"

Dorian grinned. "I say, good work! You get it open—I'll tell Ada."

Hugo started to pry open the edge of the manhole cover with his screwdriver attachment. But the tool wasn't really designed for this kind of work and broke in half just as the manhole cover came free. Hugo slid the screwdriver into his pocket, wincing. He'd have to solder it back together when he got home.

The thought of going home surprised Hugo. His quiet attic room felt so far away. The idea of going back there now and being on his own again was a bit depressing. Dorian had changed everything. He'd stomped into Hugo's life and turned it inside out. Hugo had been perfectly content before Dorian had shown him what he was missing. Now he'd never be able to forget it. Hugo wasn't sure he'd ever be able to convince himself that he was happy again.

When Dorian and Ada returned, Dorian told Hugo, "Ada's going to stay here and guard the entrance until we get back. She'll try to distract the librarian."

Dorian was clearly too much of a gentleman to say that Ada was staying here because she was far too big to fit into the sewers.

Hugo nodded and said, "But I'm not sure how we're going to get down. Look."

Dorian knelt next to Hugo to peer into the hole. Black water flowed in a stream several feet below them. There wasn't a ladder or anything to help them climb down.

Dorian sat back on his heels, frowning. "Would it be terrible if we took one of those vines?"

One of the plants growing near them had thick brown vines stretching out across the ground. Hugo looked more closely and saw that there was a diagram written on the vine showing the trading routes used in a nearby star system.

Hugo tugged at it. "It might just about hold our weight," he said. "Let's give it a try."

Dorian said, "If you wouldn't mind?" to the plant. It shivered slightly, and then the vine fell away from the plant's trunk, right into Dorian's hand.

"Much appreciated," Dorian said to the plant. He started tying the end of the vine around one of Ada's rocks.

Feeling a bit silly, Hugo whispered, "Thank you," to the plant as well. One of its small young vines reached out and tapped Hugo gently on the head.

"Better hurry," Ada said. "The librarian is sharpening her shears."

Dorian said, very quickly, "I'll go first, then." He braced his legs on the edge of the manhole and held on to the vine as he lowered himself down into blackness.

Hugo held his breath, hoping that the vine wouldn't snap and send Dorian tumbling into the rushing water below.

But Dorian made it safely down to the bottom. Then it was Hugo's turn. He gulped.

"Good luck, little one," Ada said.

"Thanks," Hugo said, feeling very worried.

Hugo found that holding his weight up with the rope was harder than it looked. Dorian had made it seem easy. Hugo ended up sliding down most of the way, flinging out his plier attachment to grip onto the vine and stop his fall. He then inched down the rest of the way and slid slowly into the water. It came up to his knees.

A shadow settled over the hole above Hugo and Dorian, leaving them in darkness. It was Ada, sitting on top of the manhole cover in case the librarian walked past.

Dorian reached out and touched Hugo's elbow. "Can you . . . have you got a light?" Dorian asked. "I don't really like the dark."

Hugo released some of his clockwork moths, which glowed in the darkness. Dorian sighed with relief.

"All right, then. Left or right?" Dorian asked.

"Left," Hugo said firmly, just because the water looked like it was a bit shallower in that direction.

They followed the curve of the sewer as it passed under the library. Sometimes they had to duck below roots hanging from the ceiling, where trees in the library had broken through the floor to stretch down to the water.

Eventually they reached a set of steps and climbed out of the water onto a brick pathway.

Hugo gasped. There was a clear pair of wet footprints heading down the tunnel. Someone had been here not long ago. What if it was the cleaning android from the footage? The one with the dark, sinister eyes? What if he was still here now?

Hugo's moths fluttered down the tunnel, lighting up the footprints with flickering glowing dots.

"Do you think that could be my cleaner?" Dorian whispered, holding out his foot to test the size next to the footprint. "It looks about the right size."

Hugo nodded. He realized his hands were trembling as his cogs whirred out of sync. What could the cleaner be doing down here? Was the cleaner storing quantum energy until he had enough to blow up the library from underground?

Hugo could just imagine an explosion tearing up from under the floor of the library, burning all the plants and killing anyone inside. It seemed so drastic. Hugo guessed the cleaner was planning to set off a bomb to make a political point. But nothing could justify *murder*.

They had to stop him.

CHAPTER 6

Hugo and Dorian followed the wet footprints down the tunnel, which split into several forks. Each turn seemed to lead them further underground. Left, then right, then left again.

"What *is* this place?" Dorian asked. "We might never find our way back out of here. It's an endless series of winding tunnels."

"I'll get us out again," Hugo said. He was memorizing the turns they took as they walked. He could picture the path like it was a layer of cogs in a watch. Getting out would be as easy as putting a watch back together from scratch—he knew he wouldn't make a mistake.

They reached a spiral staircase set into a wall and started climbing down, down, down into the ground. The rusting metal staircase rattled as they walked. Hugo winced. It felt like the staircase could collapse at any moment.

Hugo stopped at the bottom of the stairs. They were in some kind of abandoned underground church. There was a stone altar, with a rotting piece of golden fabric spread over the top. A marble statue of some ancient god with five arms stretched up toward the ceiling.

Dorian gasped. "Oh! Oh, my! I think this is the Under City!"

"The *what?*" Hugo asked.

"I thought it was just a rumor," Dorian said, amazed. "I didn't know you could still get down here!" He turned to Hugo, his eyes glowing in the light of the clockwork moths. "This planet is ancient. There have been civilizations here for thousands . . . no, *millions* of years before the academy was ever built. No one can even remember what species lived here first, because it was that long ago. The story goes that the whole planet was dead and abandoned when the academy's founders decided to build a campus here."

Hugo listened, flabbergasted. He had thought the academy was the first thing to be built on this planet.

"There's always been a rumor," Dorian continued, "well, I thought it was a rumor, anyway, that the campus was built on top of an old lost city. Instead of knocking down the buildings, the academy's founders just paved over them and built the campus on top."

"This is an old city?" Hugo asked, stunned. He peered out through an archway to see what was beyond the church. There was a small cobbled stone street stretching out toward a row of buildings.

Dorian was right. This was old—older than anything Hugo had ever seen before. And it had been totally forgotten.

Dorian followed Hugo out into the street. "The rumor said that there's another layer below this city too. The people who lived here had done the same thing before, you see. They built their city on top of another one. You can get down there from this city into one millions of years older than this place."

"Is there another city below that, and another?" Hugo asked, half joking. "Do they stretch down inside the core of the planet?"

Dorian grinned at him. "I don't know. But we could find out." Dorian laughed. "It would make a wonderful essay topic for my Historic Civilizations class. Ada would be furiously jealous."

They carried on walking around the underground city, following the trail of footprints. The footprints weren't wet and damp from the sewers anymore, but instead left scuffmarks in thousands of years of dust.

Hugo kept jumping at every shadow and noise, but he still couldn't resist peering inside buildings as they walked. He could almost tell what they had originally been—here was a bakery, and here was something that might have been a classroom. There was a swimming pool and a garden. Dorian seemed as amazed by the city as Hugo was. He must not have seen anything like this before either.

"Is your planet as old as this one?" Hugo asked. He wanted to keep talking in order to distract himself from the danger they were in.

Dorian shook his head and said, "My species lives in the ocean. Our buildings are woven from seaweed and other plants. The platforms rot away if you don't replace them. There's nothing on my planet that's more than a few decades old."

"Is it hard? Not having any record of the past like that?" Hugo asked. They pushed open a door, which collapsed into sawdust at the movement.

"I don't know," Dorian replied. "I never really thought about it until I came here and saw how solid the buildings on land are. They're so permanent. That was when I decided I wanted to give the academy a try."

"You didn't want to come here at first?"

"Not at *all*," Dorian said. "I don't really like breathing air. It's . . . messy. Like down here, breathing in all this dust. The first time I landed on this planet it was disgusting. I could smell everyone around me. It felt like I was breathing in *parts of them*."

"That does sound disgusting," Hugo admitted. He'd never thought about breathing like that, but now he was glad that he didn't have to do it.

"It is!" Dorian said. "I much prefer being below water, where I can use my gills. And I can swim, instead of doing this horrible walking thing! I'm not so clumsy then, you know. You'd find me much more impressive." Dorian twisted in a smooth spin, like he was swimming in water.

"You have *gills*?" Hugo peered at Dorian in the dim light to see if he could spot any.

Dorian stopped walking and held his breath. For a moment, nothing happened, and then little lines appeared in the sides of his neck. The gills fluttered open, searching for oxygen in the dry air. Then Dorian opened his mouth, gasping for breath, and the gills closed up.

Dorian rubbed his hands over the lines on his neck, pressing them down flat. He looked a bit embarrassed. "I've never shown them to anyone here before."

Hugo looked away, trying hard not to stare. "Thank you for showing me. They're ... beautiful."

Dorian cleared his throat, his face flushing red.

A cog inside Hugo's chest fluttered slightly.

"Anyway," Dorian said. "I settled down here, eventually. I didn't have a choice, really. My father needs me to learn the other intergalactic languages so we can increase our number of trading partners. The algae we grow on our planet is used as a food source by other people."

"That's why you're learning Ada's language?" Hugo asked.

Dorian nodded and said, "It's hard. I don't really get much time to practice, and Ada's always so busy. She helps me when she can, but she's got her own work to do. I didn't get very good scores in my last exams."

Before Hugo could reply, they both froze and stared at each other. Something ahead of them had made a noise. Hugo's fear came back in a rush. They were in danger. They shouldn't be chatting like they were out for an afternoon stroll.

Hugo clicked his fingers. His moths came fluttering back to him and landed in his palm. He put them in his pocket.

Hugo felt Dorian reach out, touching the back of his wrist, and Hugo took his hand. They stood together in the blackness, listening for the sound again.

Now that the glow from the moths had gone, Hugo could see that there was a faint light ahead of them. It must be quite far away, because it was hardly visible—just a white tinge to the edges of the darkness.

"Shall we go and see what it is?" Hugo said eventually, when they didn't hear the sound again.

Dorian squeezed his hand as a reply.

Together, they walked down the street, nearly tripping down a set of steps in the darkness. The light ahead of them grew brighter, until they turned a corner and found a . . .

A campsite.

Hugo blinked, trying to take it in. The street opened up into a square, with a fountain in the center and shops around the edges. There were dozens of tents set up in the square, and there were androids everywhere. Sitting and chatting, walking around, sweeping up. Dozens and dozens of *androids*.

The ones nearest to them spotted Hugo and Dorian. The androids froze, staring at them with wide eyes. The low murmur of conversation dropped away.

For a moment, everyone hesitated. And then the androids scattered. They turned and ran, vanishing into buildings and alleys, sprinting away as fast as possible. In only a few moments, Hugo and Dorian were alone in the square.

CHAPTER 7

"What . . . how . . . who . . . ?" Hugo stuttered as he looked around at the empty square.

"Is this some sort of android village?" Dorian whispered, sounding gobsmacked. "A city below a city, hidden under a campus?"

"Who are they?" Hugo asked. "Why are they *here?*"

Hugo slid his tool attachments out of his fingers. He held them up so he could use the sharp tips to defend himself and Dorian if someone attacked them.

"Hello there?" Dorian called out.

There was no reply. Hugo wondered if the androids were getting ready to strike.

Then Hugo heard a stifled noise that sounded like a sob. All of a sudden, Hugo felt calmer. Perhaps the androids were just as scared as they were.

"We aren't going to hurt you!" Hugo said, just in case the androids could hear him.

He and Dorian hadn't meant to scare anyone. But now Hugo realized that they were the ones who had stormed into the androids' home. They were the ones who seemed dangerous. Hugo and Dorian didn't even know if the footprints belonged to the cleaning android. These people could have nothing to do with the robberies.

Hugo turned to Dorian and said, "You stay here. If they're scared, they're more likely to trust another android. They might talk to me."

Dorian nodded. "I'll see if I can find anything around the tents. If the bomb is down here, we need to know as soon as possible so we can stop it from going off."

Hugo walked down an alley, keeping his pace slow and steady to try to show that he wasn't a threat. He extended the magnifying lens from his eye socket to make it clear that he was an android too.

Hugo spotted a shadow around the corner of an alleyway. Something scuffled ahead of him. Hugo froze and cleared his throat.

"I don't want to hurt you," he said. "I was just wondering what you were doing down here."

There was a long silence, and then an android said, "You can't make us leave. We don't have anywhere else to go."

"You . . . are you hiding?" Hugo asked. "Have they been trying to make you leave the academy?" Hugo swallowed and added, "They did that to me too. I know how it feels."

"The security guards did," the android said, and he stepped out of the shadows. Hugo saw that he was an older model from a few decades ago. His outer skin was rusted and dented, and he was missing one of his eye attachments. "They chased us all away," the android continued. "We had nowhere else to go."

Something in Hugo's chest ached as he said, "You were abandoned here too, like me, weren't you? Who was your owner? One of the students?"

"My owner was a professor," the android replied. "She upgraded to a newer model and left me here when she transferred to a different university planet. But many of us belonged to students, yes."

Hugo pulled a face. "And the security guards wouldn't let you stay at the academy without a job?" he asked.

The android nodded. "I tried to find a job. We all did. But the waiting lists are too long. There's nothing. I was chased from building to building until I found an access shaft to the Under City. No one followed me down here. I was finally left on my own. I was just planning to stay here until I reached the top of the waiting list and could get a job as a cleaner. But I stumbled into the square a few days later and found all the other androids. Some of them had been here for years. They'd found their way here, one by one."

Hugo wrapped his arms around his chest, horrified. All these androids, alone, with nothing. No one had even noticed that they'd disappeared. They'd fallen through the cracks of society and been left to hide in the dark like rats.

If Hugo hadn't been so lucky, he could have found himself down here too. If he hadn't started fixing watches, he would have been chased away from the starlight, away from life. He'd have been forgotten and abandoned in a city older than time itself.

"I'm so sorry," Hugo said to the android, meaning it deeply.

The android came closer. His entire body was shining with mirrors, which was a sign that he was running low on energy. The android was using the mirrors to desperately absorb any available traces of light, to keep himself running. He must only be a day or two from shutting down completely, as there were only a few lamps in the whole campsite.

Hugo clicked his fingers so his clockwork moths flittered back into light. The android drifted close to their glow, his mirrors twisting to face the light sources.

The android sighed and murmured, "Thank you." His eyes fluttered closed as his batteries started to charge.

Hugo had a sudden realization. "That's why you needed the quantum energy, isn't it?" he asked. "There's no starlight down here. You need the quantum energy to survive. Did you ask one of the cleaners to help you get the power you needed to recharge your batteries?"

Hugo felt utterly relieved. He had hated the thought of an android like him making a bomb. That had seemed to be the only explanation for the stolen energy, and he hadn't liked the idea that an android was capable of doing something so dangerous.

The android's eyes opened. "You can't tell anyone," he said, his cogs grinding together with panic. "They'll come down here and drive us away! We only took what we needed to survive. We didn't mean any harm."

"It's OK," Hugo said, and reached out to touch the android's arm. "I promise, it's OK. I understand. I'd have done the same."

The android frowned. "Who *are* you? What are you doing here?"

"I'm Hugo. I'm here with my friend. We were trying to find out who was taking the quantum energy. Would you like to come and meet him? Could you ask everyone to come out? I promise we're not going to hurt you."

The android nodded and said, "I'm Alfred. It's nice to meet you, Hugo." Then he whistled. Hugo jumped when what he'd thought were walls suddenly started moving—androids were stepping out of their hiding places.

Hugo shivered. He was totally surrounded. If the androids decided that Hugo was dangerous, they could destroy him in moments.

"Hi," Hugo said to the androids, trembling a little. "Um . . . you heard all that, right?"

"Do you trust the friend you're with?" a female android asked Hugo. "He's biological. Is he going to report us?"

Hugo shook his head firmly. "Dorian wouldn't. He's a good person. He'll want to help you. I know it."

CHAPTER 8

Hugo led the androids back to the square. Dorian was peering inside one of the small tents. He straightened up when he saw the androids.

"Hello!" Dorian called out. Hugo could tell that Dorian's cheeriness was fake. He was getting to know Dorian well enough to tell what he was thinking.

There were around forty androids in total—many more than Hugo had realized. They must have gotten used to hiding, even down here. They gathered around Dorian, who moved closer to Hugo, clearly feeling a bit nervous.

Hugo quickly explained to Dorian that the androids were all hiding down here because they weren't allowed on the academy campus without jobs.

"That's why they were taking the energy," he said. "There's no starlight here to give them power, so they needed another source to make sure they didn't shut down and die."

Dorian frowned. "That explains it. But surely there's somewhere you could get the energy from without *stealing*?"

Hugo thought the androids would start defending themselves. But instead of yelling, they murmured their agreement.

"I said that, back when we decided to ask the cleaners to help us," a female android said, raising her voice. She had a strange accent that Hugo didn't recognize—her owner must have come from a small, faraway planet. "Someone was bound to notice sooner or later. The quantum energy from the watches was a good plan, but it can't help us in the long run."

"We need to find a way to work on the surface," Alfred said. "We don't even have to be paid. As long as we have ID, we'll be able to get all the daylight we need."

"We must be able to help them somehow," Dorian said to Hugo. "We can't leave them down here."

"You'll help us?" the woman asked, surprised.

Dorian nodded. "Before I met Hugo, I never really thought about all the people who keep the academy running. I wish I had. I've never been friends with an android before Hugo. I didn't even know how *alive* androids could be. I'll do whatever it takes to make sure that you don't have to stay in the dark down here. You deserve better than that." Dorian cleared his throat and added, "I'm not sure how, just yet. But Hugo is clever. Much cleverer than me. I'm sure he's got lots of ideas."

Hugo stared at the androids. He felt so guilty for not thinking about them sooner. He should have known that others would have been abandoned on campus like he was. But as soon as Hugo had found a way to make money for himself, he hadn't even considered anyone else.

"Well . . . I suppose I could take one of you on as an apprentice watchmaker," Hugo said. "You could work with me, and you'd have an ID card then. You'd be allowed on campus. But the university wouldn't let me take more than one of you on as an apprentice. Maybe two."

"That's a good start!" Dorian said. "I could try to talk to the academy staff too. Surely they can hire more cleaners from the waiting list? I'll ask my father to request that the buildings be cleaned more often."

Alfred turned to the other androids and repeated what Dorian had said more loudly for the people at the back. Then he said it again in a different language.

"I say, wait a moment. You speak Hiccaran?" Dorian asked. "Can you *all* speak other languages?"

The androids nodded but looked confused.

"What languages?" Dorian asked, sounding excited. "Can anyone speak Zumian?"

A few of them raised their hands, including Alfred.

Dorian turned to Hugo. Dorian's mouth was set in a straight unreadable line, but his eyes were shining brightly. "I know what we need to do," Dorian said. "I know how we can help."

"How?!" Hugo asked.

Dorian spoke loudly so everyone could hear him. "I'm studying languages at the academy. I find it really hard, because I don't have anyone to practice with. I failed my last exams, and a lot of people in my class did too. I know for a fact that many of my friends would pay good money for language tutors. They're all training to be diplomats for their planets. It's really important for them to be fluent in lots of different languages."

"You want us to be *tutors*?" Alfred asked. "Why would the students want us to do that? They abandoned us because we're old and clumsy compared to the fancy new android models. They think we're broken bits of junk."

Dorian shook his head and said, "I think that your experience is exactly why they'd want to hire you. Hugo, how many languages did you say that you speak? Forty or so?"

Hugo nodded and replied, "Something like that." He wasn't sure what he thought of Dorian's idea, but Dorian seemed very excited about it.

"I bet you learned those as a servant, didn't you?" Dorian asked.

"Yes," Hugo said. "Whenever the earl went to a new planet, I picked up the local language."

"Well, the newer models of androids don't have that kind of experience, do they?" Dorian pointed out. "They won't have been to that many planets or picked up all the languages that you have."

"I suppose . . ." Hugo frowned. Was Dorian right? It did take a long time to train new servants. Because they were newly made, they didn't know anything at all. They learned fast, but it still took time for them to become fluent in different languages—not to mention being trained in social etiquette and cultural differences for all the galaxy's planets. Those kinds of things varied between species, so there was a lot to catch up on. Hugo remembered how long it had taken him to learn everything the earl needed him to know.

Maybe there was something in Dorian's tutoring idea.

"If the students are all training to be diplomats, then they will probably need help learning social etiquette too," Hugo suggested. "Their new androids won't know any of that. The earl once got in a lot of trouble for trying to shake hands with a person from a planet where shaking hands was a really bad insult. That type of thing would be really useful to know, wouldn't it?"

"Brilliant!" Dorian said, clapping Hugo on the back. "Of course!"

"This could actually work," the female android said, sounding stunned.

"I can set up a tutoring service," Dorian offered. "I'll tell the academy that you're all going to be working as tutors and that you need ID cards for the campus. If any of the security guards try to chase you away, you can fetch me and I'll clear it up for you. You'll get paid, too. You'll be able to rent rooms."

"There's a lot of space in my building," Hugo said. "I live on the edge of campus, but the rent is really cheap there."

Dorian was grinning excitedly. "This is going to be fun!"

Hugo smiled back at Dorian. Hugo was pleased for the androids, but part of him was sad. He had wanted to help Dorian practice his languages, but now Dorian would use one of the tutors instead. He wouldn't need Hugo anymore.

"Let's get to work!" Dorian said, clapping his hands together. He paused. "Er, how do we get back up to the surface? The tunnels weren't the best route." He made a face.

Alfred smiled and said, "There's an elevator. Follow me." He led them around the streets to a little nook in the corner of the square. There was a small metal doorway set into the stone wall.

"We think the elevator used to be a supply shaft from when they mined for stone from the Under City," Alfred explained. "It takes you straight up to the sewers below the library. Most of us are too weak to walk up all the stairs. We'd run out of power halfway there."

"Thanks," Dorian said to Alfred. "You all pack up your things. I'll get ID cards for everyone from the academy."

"I can make some lamps too," Hugo added. "They won't give out much light, but it will help you to recharge your batteries a little while we wait for the IDs."

Dorian nodded to Hugo. "Good idea. Hopefully the IDs will only take a few days, but I'll rush them along as much as possible."

Alfred clasped Dorian's hand between his own and said, "Thank you."

"I'll get you out of here. I promise," Dorian said gravely.

CHAPTER 9

As soon as the elevator doors closed, Dorian turned to Hugo with a pale face. "Can we really do this?" Dorian asked.

Hugo was startled. Dorian had seemed so confident and sure of himself. "Yes!" Hugo replied. "Of course!"

Dorian heaved out a terrified sigh. "Are you sure? Because I was just . . . making that up as I went along."

Hugo was impressed—the academy had been training Dorian well. His diplomatic skills were incredible.

Hugo squeezed Dorian's arm and tried to hide his own worry. He thought Dorian's plan was going to be difficult to pull off, but he wasn't going to say that. Dorian needed to tackle this with his usual over-confidence, otherwise it would never happen.

Hugo said, "We can do this. We've come this far, haven't we? This is just *paperwork*. It can't possibly be harder than climbing up the side of the staff building, can it?"

Dorian nodded. "OK. OK. We can do this."

The elevator creaked as they rose upward. It stopped with a jerk and Hugo sighed with relief, but the doors didn't open.

"Are they stuck?" Hugo asked.

Dorian tried to open the doors. They didn't budge.

"Try restarting the elevator," Hugo suggested.

Dorian turned the lever. The elevator made a low grinding sound and dropped a bit lower. Hugo gasped and grabbed at Dorian's arm.

"It's broken," Hugo guessed. "Isn't it?"

Dorian shook his head but didn't risk turning the lever again. "I'm not sure . . ." Dorian said. "Who knows how old this elevator is. A hundred, a thousand years old? It's hardly a surprise if it's broken."

Hugo spent a few moments imagining what would happen if they couldn't fix the elevator. They'd be stuck in a supply shaft, deep underground, for the rest of eternity. Hugo's cogs whirred as he fought against his panic.

He had to calm down so he could think properly. The elevator worked using clockwork—just like watches. If anyone could fix the machinery, it was Hugo.

"Let me try," Hugo said, and twisted his magnifying lens out of its socket. He nudged Dorian out of the way and saw there was a metal panel covering the clockwork of the elevator's mechanism. Hugo took his broken screwdriver out of his pocket—the one that had been damaged when he'd opened the manhole in the library.

Hugo unscrewed the wall panel. There were several layers of cogs inside, with a rope wrapped around the narrow metal barrel. It must turn and wind up the rope, pulling the elevator upward.

Hugo turned the winding stem of the barrel, checking that the cogs weren't dragging against each other as they rolled. They were well oiled, and nothing seemed to be broken. The ratchet and pivot all moved when he tested them. What could be causing the problem?

Hugo put pressure on the toothed gear, watching the cogs click into place on it, one after another. Ah. There it was—a tension in the rope that shouldn't be there. The rope must be caught somewhere. Perhaps it was frayed and stuck between two wheels.

He tugged at the rope. It didn't seem to be completely broken. If he could find the problem in the rope, he'd be able to fix it.

Hugo straightened up and turned to Dorian, who had been watching him work in silence.

"All right," Hugo said. "I have good and bad news. Firstly, it's not broken. We're not stuck here."

"Brilliant!" Dorian clapped Hugo on the back. "You're wasted in that attic of yours. I should take you everywhere with me. I'd be hopeless at this. They'd find me in this elevator in two weeks with nothing but a note scratched into the metal saying 'Goodbye, fair world.'"

"Well." Hugo swallowed. "I don't *think* that's going to happen."

"So what's the bad news?" Dorian asked.

"Well . . . I'm going to have to climb out of the ceiling hatch to get it working again. Could you give me a lift up?"

Dorian looked at the tiny door in the elevator's roof. "You're going up there? Are you sure?"

"It's the only way I can get at the pulleys to clear the blockage," Hugo said.

"Do you . . ." Dorian began, looking unsure. "Do you want me to do it instead?"

Part of Hugo really wanted to say yes. His gears were still grinding together with worry whenever he thought about the drop below them. It would be even worse when Hugo was perched on top of the elevator itself. But Dorian wouldn't know what to do up there.

Hugo shook his head firmly. "No. I'll do it."

He put his foot in Dorian's cupped hands and climbed up to the hatch in the ceiling of the elevator car. He unscrewed the hatch and tugged himself out onto the top of the car.

"Good luck," Dorian said, looking a bit sick.

Hugo nodded down at him through the hatch, and then made himself stand upright. He tried to pretend he wasn't standing on top of a small box balanced in midair.

Hugo grimaced as he held onto the rope holding the car in place. A lowering mechanism was attached to it. Using his clockwork moths to see, Hugo ran his hands over the length of the rope, searching for any fraying sections that might have gotten stuck in the workings.

There was a rough patch where the rope fed into the ratchet. A stray curl of rope had caught and twisted around it. Hugo used his scissors tool to carefully cut through the tangle. As soon as it was free, the rope started moving again. The car dropped, faster than Hugo had been expecting.

He stumbled, and his foot fell through the open hatch in the roof of the elevator car. He barely stopped himself from falling inside on top of Dorian.

Hugo twisted up to reach the lever and pulled on the brakes. The rope stopped unreeling, and the elevator came to a stop again.

"Are you all right?" Dorian called. There was a high note of panic in Dorian's voice as he stood on his toes trying to peer up at Hugo.

Hugo waved his hand at Dorian. "It's OK. I've fixed it," he said, cogs fluttering wildly. "Nothing to worry about!"

Dorian made a noise of disbelief. He fluttered his hands in the air, reaching up to pat at Hugo's foot, which was still dangling through the hatch.

"That should be fine now," Hugo said, climbing back into the car. Dorian helped him down.

"That was intentional, right?" Dorian asked. "That bit where you nearly fell back through the hatch?"

Hugo gulped and said, "Of course. It's an important part of the elevator-maintenance service."

Dorian rolled his eyes. "This is *not* the time for jokes, Hugo," he said, but he was grinning.

Hugo hid a smile and turned the lever again, hoping the rope wouldn't tangle in the cogs this time. The elevator car started to rise.

Dorian and Hugo looked at each other, waiting for a jolt, but the elevator moved smoothly. They made it to the top of the shaft. As soon as the doors opened, they both lunged out of the car. Hugo pressed himself against the wall of the sewers, taking a moment to recover from the dizzy feeling of being trapped somewhere so small. The wall was sturdy against Hugo's back, and after a few moments he felt he could move again.

"Come on," Dorian said, with a grim face. "I really, really need to be above ground right now."

CHAPTER 10

They had been away for so long that Ada had fallen asleep on top of the manhole in the library. Hugo had to poke at Ada's underside with one of his long attachments until she woke up and moved.

"You'll never believe what happened to us!" Dorian told Ada dramatically as Hugo clambered out of the hole. "We've had the most shocking adventure in a supply shaft! Hugo saved my life! We'd be as flat as pancakes if it wasn't for him!"

"What a hero," Ada said dryly.

"It was . . . I didn't do anything!" Hugo spluttered, frowning at Dorian. He was posing with his chest puffed out, like he was an actor in one of the plays the students put on at the end of each semester. Hugo had been to a few of them when the earl had needed someone to reserve a seat for him in the front row.

In those plays, the heroes were always brave and muscular characters. They would slay monstrous beasts from alien planets and then launch into long, dramatic monologues about it.

Before Dorian could start making such a speech about their adventure in the elevator car, Hugo said, "Dorian, that can wait. We need to tell Ada about the *androids*!"

Dorian's puffed-out chest deflated. He dropped his hand, which he'd been sweeping downward to show Ada just how fast the car had been falling.

"Oh," Dorian said. "Yes, I suppose we should."

The three of them walked to the staff building, with Dorian telling the story of their great adventure in the Under City. He added in a few details that Hugo definitely didn't remember happening. The androids sounded three times as scary as they'd actually been, and apparently a falling piece of metal had nearly chopped off Hugo's arm just at the moment he'd fixed the elevator. It was only due to Dorian's quick action that Hugo's arm had been saved.

"This Dorian fellow sounds quite the hero," Hugo joked. "I'd love to meet him."

Dorian huffed and said, "I never should have encouraged you to make jokes, Hugo. I didn't think you'd keep making them about *me*."

Hugo smiled to himself.

"So can I hire one of the android tutors?" Ada asked.

"Absolutely! You'll be our first customer," Dorian said, delighted. "At a discount, of course."

★

It took a few days for the academy to approve Dorian's new business idea. The staff had laughed at him at first, convinced that it was all a joke. It was only when Hugo had demonstrated how many languages he could speak that the staff had stopped laughing and listened properly to Dorian's proposal.

Even then, the staff kept asking if Dorian was sure that he wanted to invest his money in something so risky. They seemed convinced that the older androids were slow, stupid, and broken. It made Hugo realize how much the staff looked down on the androids who applied to be cleaners. No wonder the waiting list for jobs was so long. The staff at the academy hadn't wanted to hire the older androids at all.

Dorian insisted that he wanted to go ahead with the plan, and the academy finally agreed to give the androids ID cards to the campus. But they told Dorian he would have to pay the rent up-front for the whole of Hugo's building for the next year, so the androids would have somewhere to live.

Dorian secretly tried to pay for Hugo's rent too, but Hugo noticed in time and managed to stop him. Hugo didn't want Dorian to pay for anything for him. He made enough money from his watches. Hugo wanted to be Dorian's friend, not his employee.

While they were waiting for the androids' ID cards, Hugo repaired Dorian's and Ada's watches in time for their time-travel exam. Then he also built some lamps to take down to the Under City so the androids could recharge their batteries.

A week after Dorian had gotten approval for the business, he was given the ID cards for the androids.

Hugo and Dorian took the stack of fresh ID cards to the library and called the androids out of the sewers. They soon filled the narrow aisles of the library as Dorian handed out the IDs.

Dorian led the group of androids outside, and Hugo noticed that every student stopped to stare at the dusty, rusted old androids walking past. Dorian just grinned at the students, raising one hand in a lazy salute.

"I think you came just in time," Alfred admitted to Dorian as all the androids followed Hugo to their new home in his building. "Even with the lamps that Hugo brought to us, we were close to shutting down."

The androids were walking with their faces tilted up toward the sky, absorbing as much starlight as possible.

Hugo's normally empty building was soon buzzing with life. The androids were suddenly more lively, now that they were fully charged. Hugo didn't think he'd ever feel lonely in his attic again.

"Well," Dorian said, looking around the rooms. "The androids all seem to be settling in well."

Ada was sitting outside with one of the androids, having her first tutoring session. From the attic, Hugo could hear her rumbling voice through three floors.

"I suppose I'd better leave all of you to it," Dorian said.

"Right," Hugo said, and he tried to hide how sad he was that his adventure with Dorian was over. It had been a lot of work, but he'd never felt so alive.

"I've told everyone in my class about the new tutors," Dorian said to Alfred, who had the room next to Hugo's. "The language exams start next week. I bet they'll all come running over here."

"Thank you so much for all your help," Alfred said. "If this works, you'll have changed our lives forever."

Dorian nodded calmly, but his antennae were fluttering with emotion. "I promise I won't abandon you," Dorian said. "Once this business is up and running, you'll be able to live here for the rest of your lives, if you want. I will find a way to hire every unemployed android on this planet." Dorian's eyes met Hugo's. "I promise."

Then Dorian clapped his hands together and added, "I suppose I should go and study. I haven't done much at all in the last week!"

Hugo followed Dorian outside. "Good luck with the rest of your exams," Hugo mumbled. There was so much he wanted to say to Dorian now that he was leaving. But none of the words could find their way out of Hugo's throat. "I know you'll be brilliant," Hugo said.

Dorian hesitated, then leaned in and hugged Hugo tightly. "You're the one who's brilliant. I didn't expect any of this to happen when I first came to your attic. What a great end to the term! I'll see you soon, OK?"

With one last wave, Dorian turned and left, grinning like he was filled with excited energy and new ideas. Hugo stood on the doorstep and watched him go, trying not to feel like he'd been left behind.

CHAPTER 11

At first, it was a relief for Hugo to be back in his attic room. He could finally get back to tinkering with the broken watch he'd been fixing when Dorian had knocked angrily at his door.

Hugo found it peaceful to just sit quietly at his desk after the mad rush of the last couple of weeks. He opened up the back of the watch as the fluttering wings of his glowing clockwork moths surrounded him.

Hugo pulled his magnifying lens out of his eye. One of the delicate metal cogs inside the watch had a single curl of gold sticking up from its smooth edge. A small thing, but it must have caught in the workings as the cogs turned, twisting the whole thing out of shape. Hugo opened one of the drawers in his desk and chose a new golden cog from a velvet-lined compartment.

It was almost impossible for biological people to do the kind of work that Hugo did. The cogs were so tiny that even just the throb of blood pulsing through veins could push a watchmaker's touch off course. There were biological watchmakers, of course, but they had to train themselves to work in the spaces between their heartbeats.

Hugo wondered if any of the androids would like to work for him, just as he'd offered, even though he wouldn't be able to pay as much as the students could. Hugo had never considered taking on an apprentice before, but now his attic felt cold and empty and dark, especially when he could hear the cheerful laughter of everyone chatting and joking as they set up their new rooms.

Hugo slid the new cog into place with a pair of tweezers, twisting the screw until it slipped into its socket with a tiny *click*. He turned the handle, and the cogs moved smoothly again.

He smiled. All fixed.

Hugo would have to teach Dorian a bit of watchmaking when he came to visit. Dorian didn't even understand the difference between springs and gears. He was the kind of person who found all new things interesting, so Hugo thought he'd probably love to learn about his work.

Hugo wondered when Dorian would come and visit him. He'd probably be busy for a few days with the rest of his exams. Maybe after the exams were finished, Hugo could walk over to Dorian and Ada's building and ask if they'd like to go for a walk around the academy's lake.

Hugo guessed that Dorian would go off-planet for the school break, but Dorian would have to come by the building before then to check on the androids. Hugo could invite him inside for a cup of tea. He couldn't wait.

★

Three days passed by, and Dorian still hadn't come to visit Hugo. As time went on, Hugo started to wonder if he would ever stop by the little attic room again. Maybe Dorian didn't need

Hugo anymore now that he had a whole building of androids to talk to.

On the fifth day without any news from Dorian, Hugo was utterly miserable. He couldn't bring himself to repair any of the watches that had been dropped off in his room. Hugo just stared out of the window, pretending he wasn't waiting for Dorian's familiar figure to stride down the path.

Hugo would have gone to visit Dorian himself, but as the days went by, he started to wonder if he'd imagined their friendship. What if Dorian was just being polite to Hugo? What if he hadn't really liked Hugo at all? Maybe Hugo had been annoying. Maybe it had been a relief to Dorian to get rid of him.

What if Hugo went to visit Dorian and he opened the door with a look of annoyance or, even worse, fake pleasure at the sight of him?

Hugo could just imagine an awkward, polite afternoon tea with Dorian, where they sat in silence or perhaps discussed the weather. It would be horrific. Hugo didn't want to think of it. It was much better not to visit at all than to suffer that.

They'd had one fun, exciting adventure together. That was all. That should be enough, more than enough—it was more than Hugo had ever dreamed of. He should try to be glad that it had happened at all, rather than upsetting himself by greedily wishing it had turned into something more.

Hugo looked around his tiny, worn attic. It was the same as it had always been, yet he felt too big to fit inside it anymore. His time with Dorian had changed him, filling him up from the inside with something new and exciting. It felt impossible to return to his old quiet life now.

Dorian had barged into Hugo's life and changed everything. Then he'd left again like nothing had happened.

Hugo sighed and stared down at the inside of a broken watch. He felt exhausted all of a sudden. He considered lying on his bed and letting his gears wind down for a few hours until he felt able to face the world again.

But Hugo knew he should finish the watch first, before one of the tiny cogs rolled off the desk and was lost forever. He was trying to summon up the energy to do it when there was a knock on his door. Hugo looked up, surprised.

It was Dorian. He didn't barge in angrily like the first time, demanding all of Hugo's attention. Dorian just hovered in the entrance. He looked nervous.

"Hello again," Dorian said. "I was wondering . . ." He stopped talking and cleared his throat.

Hugo stood up. He could hear his cogs whirring fast, but it felt like it was happening somewhere very far away.

Hugo saw that Dorian was holding a small plant pot.

Dorian seemed to notice it at the same time as Hugo, because he held out his hands and pushed the plant into Hugo's chest.

Hugo carefully touched one of the flowers. It felt as thin as paper and too delicate to touch. He'd never had a plant before.

"It reminded me of your tattoos," Dorian said shyly, reaching out to touch Hugo's arm.

Hugo looked down and saw that all his tattoos were frantically blossoming, covering his skin in colorful flowers.

"Oh," Hugo said. The words came out a bit husky with shock. "Thank you. What are you . . . Dorian, your exams, are they . . . ?"

"The exams have been fine so far. Never mind them. I needed to make sure . . ." Dorian stopped and sighed, then continued, "The last few days, I've realized . . . I miss you. I like being your friend. And I wish we had more time to spend together, but I'm going home for the holidays soon, so I was wondering . . . I know we have only just met, but . . . do you think you might . . . ?"

Dorian stopped again, like the sentence was a cog wound down as far as it could go.

Hugo tried to finish it for him. "Come with you?"

Dorian nodded, his eyes filled with relief.

"I won't be your servant," Hugo said firmly. "I'm happy as a watchmaker, thank you very much."

"Oh! Of course, that's not what I meant."

"But . . . I could be your . . . friend?" Hugo offered.

Dorian smiled. It was a shaky, quiet sort of smile. "I would like that a lot," he said.

Hugo looked down at his plant. He should give it some water. Put it by the window, in the starlight. Plants didn't need much to survive. Just a little bit of care and attention. Just like the androids.

There was a short silence. Someone cheered downstairs, and there was the sound of laughter.

Dorian rubbed the back of his neck and said, "My home planet is very beautiful. I think you'll like it there."

Hugo beamed at him. "I'm sure I will." Hugo normally spent the holidays alone on the campus, replacing broken parts in his body. Going to Dorian's planet sounded much better.

"We can go swimming in the great coral reefs on the moon, and dive down into the thousand-league caverns underneath my father's estate," Dorian said. "Oh, watchmaker. I've got so much to show you!"

The cogs in Hugo's chest whirred into motion. He felt like he was filled to the brim with glowing starlight. His life had changed so much since he'd met Dorian. Somehow, he didn't think he'd be lonely ever again.

Our books are tested
for children and young people by
children and young people.

Thanks to everyone who consulted on
a manuscript for their time and effort in
helping us to make our books better
for our readers.

HUGO, DORIAN, AND ADA'S ADVENTURES CONTINUE...